SWEETSPIRE LITERATURE
MANAGEMENT

Dedication

For my granddaughters
Maia and Israh Harcourt

Contents

THE WITCH WHO LOST HER MAGIC
by Margaret Harcourt West
Illustrated by Hilbert Bermejo

Once upon a time there lived a witch who was very upset because she had lost her magic. As she sat on a bench among the trees, she was crying so much that her tears fell on to the grass. Her magic had been stolen by Gerald the Giant, and he would not give it back to her, no matter how many times she asked. The witch's name was Winifred the Wonder Witch, but when she used her magic, she could change into another person with another name. She could be Queen Winifred, or Princess Madeleine, or Princess Isabella, or she could be Dottie the Doll or Tom the Tiger. She could even look like a monster if she wanted to. But now she could only look like a witch, because she had lost her magic.

Gerald the Giant stole her magic, because he thought that he could use it to make everyone love him, just as they loved Winifred. And everyone did love Winifred, a good, and almost pretty witch, who was kind and caring; and who loved to help people who were in trouble. Unlike grumpy Gerald, Winifred was a happy person, and when her big brown eyes twinkled and she smiled her big toothy smile, everyone just loved her. Nobody loved Gerald the Giant, because he just sat in his castle and ate too much and drank too much, and was grumpy with everyone around him. The only person who loved Gerald was his wife Gina, and even she kept saying: 'Get off the chair Gerald! Why don't you go out there and do some good deeds!'

As for Winifred, she was always helping people. Once some children were planting trees and they all sat down, because they were too tired to plant any more. Winifred felt sorry for them, and with three spells and two turns with her broom, she planted three hundred trees. Just like that!

Another time she saw that some kangaroos were looking very sad, because they had lost part of their forest. It had all been cleared, because some people needed to build a golf course. Straight away, Winifred said: 'Don't worry, you beautiful kangaroos, I can help you.' She turned around six times, muttered three spells, and waved her broom in the air. Magically, the forest returned, so the kangaroos had their home back.

But Winifred couldn't plant trees, or recreate the forest anymore, because she had lost her magic. Poor Winifred! She couldn't even fly! She was so upset, she just sat on a bench and cried and cried, because she just didn't know what to do. Then after one more cry, Winifred dried her eyes and went for a walk in the forest, where it was quiet and peaceful, and she could think about her problem.

She was sitting beneath a very tall eucalyptus tree, when she thought of an answer. 'I know what I can do,' she thought. 'I'll ask Leonardo the Lion for help. He owes me a favour, and he did promise to help if ever I were in trouble.' As she began to walk on through the forest, Winifred thought about the time she had helped Leonardo the Lion.

Leonardo and his wife Lucy were Gerald the Giant's pet lion cubs, and he loved them and cuddled them and let them roam through his castle. Unfortunately they grew into huge lions, and they soon became the parents of three little lion cubs. There were now far too many lions for Gerald to manage, so he told them he was very sorry, but they would all have to go and live in the zoo.

Winifred heard about her friend Leonardo's problem, and she decided to solve it for him. With the help of Gina the Giant, she was able to persuade Gerald to build a wall around the lions' part of the forest. This meant that the lion family didn't have to go to the zoo, and the lions had their very own home behind the wall. The wall also meant that all the other animals, such as the kangaroos and the wallabies, felt safe from the lions.

'Yes, Leonardo the Lion owes me a favour,' thought Winifred. 'After all, I saved him from going to the zoo! I also helped him find his own home, so maybe he will help me to get my magic back.' As she neared the walled part of the forest, Winifred saw the little lion cubs playing near the gate. She unlocked the gate with her secret key, and she asked the lion cubs to take her to their father.

'Hello Winifred,' said Leonardo. 'You look very worried. What is the matter?'

'Gerald the Giant stole my magic,' she answered, 'and there's no way I can get it back again. I just don't know what to do!'

'I think I may be able to help you,' said Leonardo. 'I will take you to see Gerald the Giant, and I will make sure he gives you back your magic.'

And so Leonardo the Lion and Winifred the Wonder Witch walked out of the lions' part of the forest, and into a much thicker forest. The forest animals and reptiles, such as the wallabies and the lizards, were not frightened of the lion, because they knew that Winifred would protect them from any danger. (Little did they know that she didn't have her magic).

Winifred made sure that Leonardo walked on the path through the forest, and she kept him busy chatting about his beautiful family. Soon they came to Gerald's enormous castle.

Leonardo knew for certain that he would be welcomed by Gerald the Giant, as not only was he his pet, but he had also saved his life. Once two hundred foxes had attacked Gerald, and they almost pulled out all his hair! If it hadn't been for the strength and bravery of Leonardo, the foxes might have had Gerald for dinner! Naturally, Gerald was very grateful to Leonardo for saving his life.

Leonardo looked very confident when he knocked on the big black door, but Winifred looked very worried. Very slowly, Gina the Giant opened the door and said: 'Welcome Leonardo! Do come in. I know Gerald will be very pleased to see you, but I'm not sure about your friend Winifred the Wonder Witch. Gina took them up the stairs, through the kitchen, down some steps, and into Gerald the Giant's lounge room.

'Welcome Leonardo,' said Gerald. 'I'm always pleased to see you. But I'm not very happy to see you Winifred. You have probably come to ask for your magic to be returned.'

'Indeed she has,' said Leonardo. 'She is very, very unhappy without her magic. She can't even fly, and what is a witch if she can't fly? I beg you Gerald; please return the magic to Winifred.'

'As a matter of fact,' answered Gerald, 'I couldn't even work the magic. It is no use to me, so Winifred can have it. But if she does want it returned to her, she can work for it. Now come with me into my secret room.'

Gerald took Leonardo and Winifred down some more steps, and into a small room lined with very tall cupboards, and in the cupboards were hundreds and hundreds of coloured boxes. 'Now, in these boxes,' said Gerald, 'there are many different things. In some boxes, there are seeds of giant trees Gina wants me to plant. In others, there are some of my secrets. Among them all is the mystery box, containing Winifred's magic. You, Winifred the Wonder Witch, have to guess which box the magic is in.'

'If I don't guess the correct box, what happens?' asked Winifred.

'Then you will leave without your magic,' replied Gerald.

Winifred looked very worried, as she sighed and stared at the hundreds of boxes. 'How can I possibly pick the right box?' she asked Leonardo. 'There are hundreds of them!'

'You can do it Winifred,' replied Leonardo.

Winifred took a deep breath as she quietly, slowly, put her hands on a yellow, and then a green box. She closed her eyes, walked up and down, stopped, and counted to ten: 'One, two, three, four, five, six, seven, eight, nine, ten.'

She opened her eyes, and she found that she was looking at a red box. Straight away, she pulled it out and gave it to Gerald. 'This one,' she said.

'Thank you Winifred. But perhaps it's not the red one. I'll be kind, and let you have another try,' offered Gerald.

'No Gerald, I don't want another try. Please, just open up the box,' asked Winifred.

'All right Winifred. But I think you'll be sorry,' replied Gerald.

Slowly, Gerald removed all the gold ribbon, and all the red tape, and all the red paper - and lifted up the lid of the red box. There it was, Winifred's magic, all wrapped up in a giant, blue silk handkerchief!

Winifred was so excited to see her magic again, she hugged the Giant on his ankle, and she kissed Leonardo on his mane. 'Thank you, thank you Gerald the Giant, and thank you Leonardo the Lion,' she squealed excitedly. 'If ever I can help you, just shout, "Help, Help Winifred" four times, and then say, "Super Super Broom" five times, and I will hear you.'

Just so she could check her magic was all there, Winifred decided to change herself into a queen, before she flew away. She whispered the correct words, but nothing happened.

'That's strange,' she said to Gerald, 'I just tried to change myself into a queen, but the magic didn't work. Not that I really want to be a queen, or anyone else for that matter. I'm very happy being Winifred the Wonder Witch. Just as I am. Just me.'

'Try walking,' suggested Leonardo, 'because you once told me that you sometimes had to move to make the magic work.'

'All right, I'll try moving,' she said as she slowly walked to the big black door.

Magically, the door opened by itself, and outside the door were five broomsticks; all doing a dance, especially for Winifred. 'Broomsticks! Stop dancing and stay still!' she commanded. Immediately, they stopped dancing, and Winifred watched as the five broomsticks all blended together, to make just one broomstick!

'That's strange, the door and the broomsticks certainly know there is magic somewhere,' said Winifred. 'Let's try that magic again,' she whispered as she closed her eyes. 'I wish, I wish, I wish I were – a big, green – monster!' There was a flash and a whoosh; and when Winifred opened her eyes she saw that she was a big, green, funny monster, with five eyes, a smiley mouth, three arms, and twenty toes!

'Just testing,' said Winifred to Gerald and Leonardo, as she smiled and happily changed herself back into Winifred the Wonder Witch.

Then before Leonardo or Gerald could say M-A-G-I-C spells magic, Winifred was on her broomstick and flying high, high up to the sky. She flew through all the clouds, and on and up to her witch house, far, far away, on the highest and fluffiest cloud in the sky.

And there she stayed, for a long, long time.

THE END

SAVING THE DRAGONS
by Margaret Harcourt West
Illustrated by Hilbert Bermejo

Once upon a time there lived two bright and beautiful princesses, called Princess Madeleine and Princess Isabella. They lived in an enormous castle that overlooked a sparkling sky-blue lake. The castle was five storeys high, and it had a number of turrets from which there was a magnificent view of the lake and the surrounding forest.

Now, the princesses were very happy and busy in their castle, but they also liked to go for long walks, either in the gardens, or in the forest near the castle. One day, on their walk, they heard that there were not many dragons left in the world. The princesses already knew this, because they had an uncle and aunt who owned a zoo called, 'The Zoo for all Dragons who are Hunted, Homeless or Orphaned.' They really respected their uncle and aunt for trying to save the dragons, but the princesses wanted to help in their own way.

'I know what we could do,' said Princess Madeleine to her parents. 'We could save the dragons by having some as pets. Please, can we have two dragons each? We promise to look after them.' King Laurence and

Queen Lydia thought this was an excellent idea, as the princesses would not only be helping to save the dragons, but they would have pets they could look after and take for long walks.

And so it was that the princesses were given two dragons each as a Christmas present. They named the boy dragons George and Gawain, after knights who had fought dragons a long time ago. The girl dragons were called Gwyneth and Genevieve.

The pet dragons were so happy in the castle, they never even thought about breathing fire. Indeed, they soon forgot how it was done. 'There's no need for our dragons to breathe fire,' said Princess Madeleine. 'That's only for angry dragons, not pet dragons like ours.' 'Yes,' said Princess Isabella. 'Our dragons would much rather sleep and dream on their dragon- beds , or go for walks, or play ball games with us.'

One day Princess Madeleine was taking George and Gwyneth for a walk in the garden, and Princess Isabella was looking after Gawain and Genevieve. They heard a whooshing noise in the sky, and they looked up to see hundreds of blue witches, flying fast and high on their broomsticks. Gawain looked very worried, so Isabella said to him: 'Oh don't worry Gawain. They're just the blue witches who fly over the castle, at four o'clock every Thursday. I think they are on their way to visit their cousins on an island in the lake.'

'Oh that's all right then,' said Gawain, as he and the other dragons started to play a ball game.

Unbeknown to the princesses and the dragons, the blue witches had noticed the pet dragons playing in the garden.

'Dragons!' screeched Zamia, the second leader of the blue witches. 'Let's fly down right now, and pick them up. I've always wanted to ride on a dragon, and go zooming through the sky.' 'Yes,' said Zemira, the leader of the blue witches. 'That would be a lot more fun than riding on a broomstick. But we don't have time to collect the dragons. Our cousins on the island are expecting us to be there at five o'clock.'

'Couldn't we be just a little bit late?' asked Zamia.

'No Zamia, we couldn't. We'll pick up the dragons some other time,' replied Zemira.

'Is that a promise?' asked Zamia.

'Yes, Zamia, it is a promise,' answered Zemira, as she flew even faster.

A few days later, on a warm and sunny day, the princesses were reading a story to their pet dragons.

They had reached a very exciting part of the story, when they looked up to the sky (and there they were) the blue witches! 'Oh look Isabella, they're carrying baskets!' yelled Madeleine. 'You know I heard Uncle Van say that blue witches like to steal dragons. He said they put them in baskets, and then they use the dragons like broomsticks - to fly through the sky.'

'I don't believe you Madeleine. You're just trying to scare me.' shouted Isabella.

'Well - just in case it's true,' said Madeleine, 'let's get our dragons inside the castle.

You can deal with Gwyneth and Gawain, and I'll chase up George and Genevieve.'

As the princesses were busy calling their dragons, they noticed that thousands and thousands of dandelions were falling from the sky. The whole of the garden was yellow with dandelions, and the smell of them was very powerful. So powerful, that the girls and the dragons became very, very sleepy, and they lay down on the yellow petals to sleep.

The blue witches were flying in the sky above, and they were all thinking how clever they were, to think of a dandelion-sleeping-spell.

'It worked! It worked!' shouted Zamia. 'The dragons and the princesses are sound asleep. All we have to do is put the dragons in our baskets, and there'll be no wriggling and squiggling, because they'll be asleep. Easy peasy.'

'There's no hurry Zamia,' said Zemira. 'They'll be asleep for a long, long time, so we can fly to the island first; then we can pick up the dragons on our way home.'

'Oh no! I want to pick them up right now!' screamed Zamia. But then she sighed, and said:

'But I suppose you're right. It makes more sense to pick them up on the way home.'

Hours later, Princess Madeleine woke up, and saw that the dragons and Princess Isabella were still asleep. 'Wake up Isabella,' said Madeleine. 'Quick, we've got to get our dragons into the castle, before the blue witches come back.' Isabella would not wake up, so Madeleine tickled her with some leaves. She woke up with a start.

'Look Madeleine!' she exclaimed, 'the dragons are still here. I dreamt that the blue witches took them away.'

'Yes, they are here, but they are asleep, and they are much too heavy for us to carry into the castle. I could try tickling them with leaves, and they might wake up. Just the way you did, when I tickled you with some leaves.'

'I've got another idea,' giggled Isabella. 'I'll get some pepper, so they can sniff it, and then they'll sneeze so hard they'll wake up.'

So Madeleine tickled the dragons with leaves, and Isabella made them sniff the pepper. But no, the dragons slept on and on, as if they had no intention of ever waking up. The princesses tried to lift them, but they were just too heavy.

The princesses were so sad, they were about to cry, when suddenly Madeleine jumped up and shouted: 'Isabella! Isabella! I've just remembered what Daddy said about Gerald the Giant and Gina, coming to visit us today!'

'That's right,' said Isabella. 'They will be here today. I'm sure they will help us.'

'Of course they will,' said Madeleine. 'They have dragons of their own, and they know there are not many dragons left in the world. They would definitely want to help us to save our dragons.'

'That's true,' said Isabella thoughtfully. 'Gerald is such a kind giant now. He used to be very grumpy, but since Gina made him go outside and plant trees, and do good deeds, he's turned into a super nice giant. I know he will help us.'

Just as the princesses were talking about Gerald the Giant, a flying figure with green curly hair appeared in the sky.

'We're saved, Isabella! Look, there's our magic friend, Winifred the Wonder Witch!' yelled Madeleine.

'She's making a surprise visit! Just when we need her!' exclaimed Isabella.

'And look! Gerald and Gina are coming over the hill!' shouted Madeleine, as she and Isabella jumped for joy.

After the princesses had hugged Winifred, and Gerald and Gina, Madeleine said excitedly: 'You have arrived just in time. We can't lift the dragons because they're asleep, and they're too heavy; and we need to get them inside the castle, before the blue witches steal them.'

'Yes, I have heard that the blue witches like to steal dragons; but it could be just a story,' said Gerald.

'No, it's true Gerald!' exclaimed Winifred. 'And, my beautiful princesses, that's why I came to warn you. I actually heard the blue witches saying they want to steal some dragons. They want to use them, like broomsticks, to ride through the sky. Quick, let me put a spell on your dragons and wake them up. Then, in a flash, I could whisk them inside the castle.'

'No Winifred. Let them sleep,' said Gerald. 'I can carry them very easily. It's no trouble.' He then picked up George and Gwyneth and carried them inside the castle. He had just returned for Gawain and Genevieve, when he noticed crowds of blue witches whizzing through the sky.

'Well, double my broomsticks! Just look at that ladies! Gerald the Giant is carrying away the very last of the dragons. So now what do we do?' asked Zemira.

'I know what to do!' exclaimed Zamia. 'Don't you see? If Gerald and Gina are inside the princesses' castle; that means that their dragons are all alone. This is the perfect time to fly to Gerald's castle, pick up his dragons, and Billy's your broomstick! Easy peasy.'

'Zamia, you've had ideas before, and they didn't work out,' sighed Zemira. 'But this time, they just might. Turn around ladies. Off we go to the castle of Gerald the Giant.' And whoosh! Whee! All the blue witches were up and zooming through the sky.

Meanwhile, inside the castle, Winifred, and Gerald and Gina, were drinking some of the princesses' peppermint tea.

'Madeleine and Isabella,' said Winifred, 'don't worry about your dragons. They'll be awake in a few hours, and they won't even remember what happened. But I must go now, and see what those nasty blue witches are up to. Thank you for the tea. 'Bye everyone!'

As Winifred the Wonder Witch was about to close the front door of the castle, she looked up to the sky, and she saw the blue witches. They were flying hurriedly away - in the direction of Gerald the Giant's castle.

'Oh no!' exclaimed Winifred, 'they are probably going to steal Gerald's dragons. I must get to his castle before they do.'

She called to Gerald and Gina to go home as quickly as they could. Then faster than lightning, she flew on her broomstick to the giants' castle.

As soon as she arrived, Winifred ran into the giants' kitchen, where ten dragons were eating their meal of meat and potatoes.

'Dragons, hurry, hurry!' she shouted. 'Get up on the roof and try to find your fire! The blue witches are coming, and they are going to steal you away, and use you, like broomsticks, to ride through the sky. Quickly, find your anger! Find your fire, and blow them all away!'

Now, Gerald the Giant's dragons were just like those belonging to Princess Madeleine and Princess Isabella. They had lost their fire, and they couldn't breathe fire, unless they were very, very angry. But at the thought of being stolen by the blue witches, and being swapped for broomsticks, they suddenly began to feel quite, angry. Angry enough to go up on the roof of the castle. And by the time they had climbed the stairs and reached the roof, they were feeling very, angry. And by the time they had settled down, and found their place on the roof, they were feeling very, very angry!

Winifred and the dragons looked up at the sky, and they saw all the blue witches, many with black dragon-cages, swinging on their broomsticks.

'Now!' shouted Winifred, 'find your fire! And if you do, I will cast a spell, and the fire will be three times bigger. It will be so big, the blue witches will be absolutely terrified, and they will never, never come near you again.'

After listening to Winifred the Wonder Witch, all the dragons took a long, long, long dragon—breath- and there it was! Fire! Fantastic, flaming fire, coming from the mouths of all ten dragons!

Then it was Winifred's turn to cast her spell, and suddenly the fire was so ferocious, it filled the sky with a burning furnace-red, and it seemed as if the whole world were on fire. Giant flames whizzed towards the sky, and frightened the blue witches so much, that they dropped their cages. Terrified of the raging fire, they flew back up to the clouds, faster than you could say: 'dragon-fire.'

As quickly as it had come, the ferocious fire vanished, and there was not even a wisp of smoke in the air. Instead of breathing fire, the dragons were now all smiling and happy - and very proud of the way they had fought off the blue witches.

'Yes, Dragons, you did very well. But don't forget you could have been the blue witches' broomsticks, if it hadn't been for me,' said Winifred.

'Oh yes, thank you Winifred,' cried all the dragons.

'From all of us, thank you, you amazing Wonder Witch,' added the biggest of the dragons. And because he wanted to show Winifred just how much he loved her, the biggest dragon suddenly picked her up, tossed her in the air, and entwined her in his enormous tail.

Winifred was feeling a little breathless, and was just about to call out, "Help! Help! Super-Super broom!" when Gerald and Gina, and Princess Madeleine, and Princess Isabella, appeared on the roof. 'Enough,' said Gerald to the biggest dragon. 'Let her go. We all love Winifred the Wonder Witch, and we would never want to lose her.' The biggest dragon let go of Winifred, and she could breathe properly again. Then everyone (except the dragons) gave her the biggest and best hug she had ever had in her life.

'Quiet everyone!' shouted Princess Madeleine, as Gerald lifted her onto his shoulders. 'I think we should celebrate the saving of our dragons. So, you are all invited to our castle - for a party! If it is all right with our parents, the party will be next Thursday, at three o'clock.' 'Oh yes!' exclaimed Princess Isabella. 'Do come everyone. I promise you, it will be the best party, with the most fun, and the yummiest party food you have ever tasted.'

The day of the party arrived, and the castle and the grounds were packed with people. The pet dragons entertained them with a dragon-race, which, much to her surprise, was won by Genevieve. Madeleine wanted to tell Winifred about Genevieve's win. But where was Winifred ? Madeleine spotted her under a tree nearby. She was crying so hard that all her tears fell on to the grass. 'Sorry Madeleine,'said Winifred. 'I'm crying because

I'm so happy. Just like the sad time I cried when I had lost my magic. When I'm too sad or too happy - I cry.' 'Oh Winifred, our precious precious Winifred, I just love you,' Madeleine whispered as she gave Winifred the biggest hug. 'But come on now. Let's get back to the party ....and the food!'

As Princess Isabella had promised, the food was the yummiest party food, anyone had ever tasted.

This was the menu:

Pizza, muffins,

chocolate cake, cupcakes,

carrot cake, fairy bread, bananas,

strawberries, cherries, peaches, pears,

rock melon, ice cream, fruit salad,

apples, plums, yoghurt; and lots of

different milkshakes.

All the guests agreed, the party was the perfect way to
celebrate - the saving of the dragons.

THE END